C2 000001 981614 6X

Retold by Polly Lawson
First published in German under the title *Ein Märchen im Sommerwald*

British Library CIP Data available
ISBN 0-86315-174-4 Printed in Belgium

The Pancake that Ran Away

A picture book by
Loek Koopmans

Floris Books

There were once three old ladies who liked nothing better than meeting for a good old chat together. So one fine spring morning there they were chatting away, when they got a sudden longing for pancakes.

"Let's meet at my house," said one of the old ladies. "Bring flour, fat, milk and eggs. We'll have a pancake party."

But when the first old lady went home, she found she had only flour and fat, no milk or eggs.

"I'll provide the flour and the fat," cried the first old lady.

The second old lady found she had no eggs or flour. She had only milk.
"I'll provide the milk," cried the second old lady.

The third old lady had no milk or flour. She had only one egg.
"I'll provide the egg," cried the third old lady.

Then she heated up the stove and waited for her friends. Together they mixed the dough and then they put the pan on the stove.

"Mmm, mmm," said the three old ladies as they watched the pancake sizzling in the pan.

"Let's toss the pancake," said the three old ladies. One of them took the pan in her hand.

Then what a surprise! The pancake leapt out of the pan and started to roll towards the door. "You can't catch me," the pancake cried.

The three old ladies stood laughing and laughing. They had never seen anything like it before.

"You can't catch me," the pancake cried.
And it rolled away into the woods as fast as it could go.

The pancake came to a little hen who cried out, “Stop, you lovely fat pancake, I’d like to eat you up.”

"Oh, yes," replied the pancake, "you'd like that, wouldn't you. But three old ladies can't catch me, and neither will you!"

Soon the pancake rolled past a dog who cried out, “Stop, you lovely fat pancake, I’d like to eat you up.”

"Oh, yes," replied the pancake, "you'd like that, wouldn't you. But three old ladies can't catch me, a little hen can't catch me, and neither will you!"

Then the pancake rolled past a large pig who cried out, “Stop, you lovely fat pancake, I’d like to eat you up.”

"Oh, yes," replied the pancake, "you'd like that, wouldn't you. But three old ladies can't catch me, a little hen can't catch me, a dog can't catch me, and neither will you!"

After a bit the pancake rolled past a goat who cried out, "Stop, you lovely fat pancake, I'd like to eat you up."

"Oh, yes," replied the pancake, "you'd like that, wouldn't you. But three old ladies can't catch me, a little hen can't catch me, a dog can't catch me, a pig can't catch me, and neither will you!"

Next the pancake rolled past a horse who cried out, "Stop, you lovely fat pancake, I'd like to eat you up."

"Oh, yes," replied the pancake, "you'd like that, wouldn't you. But three

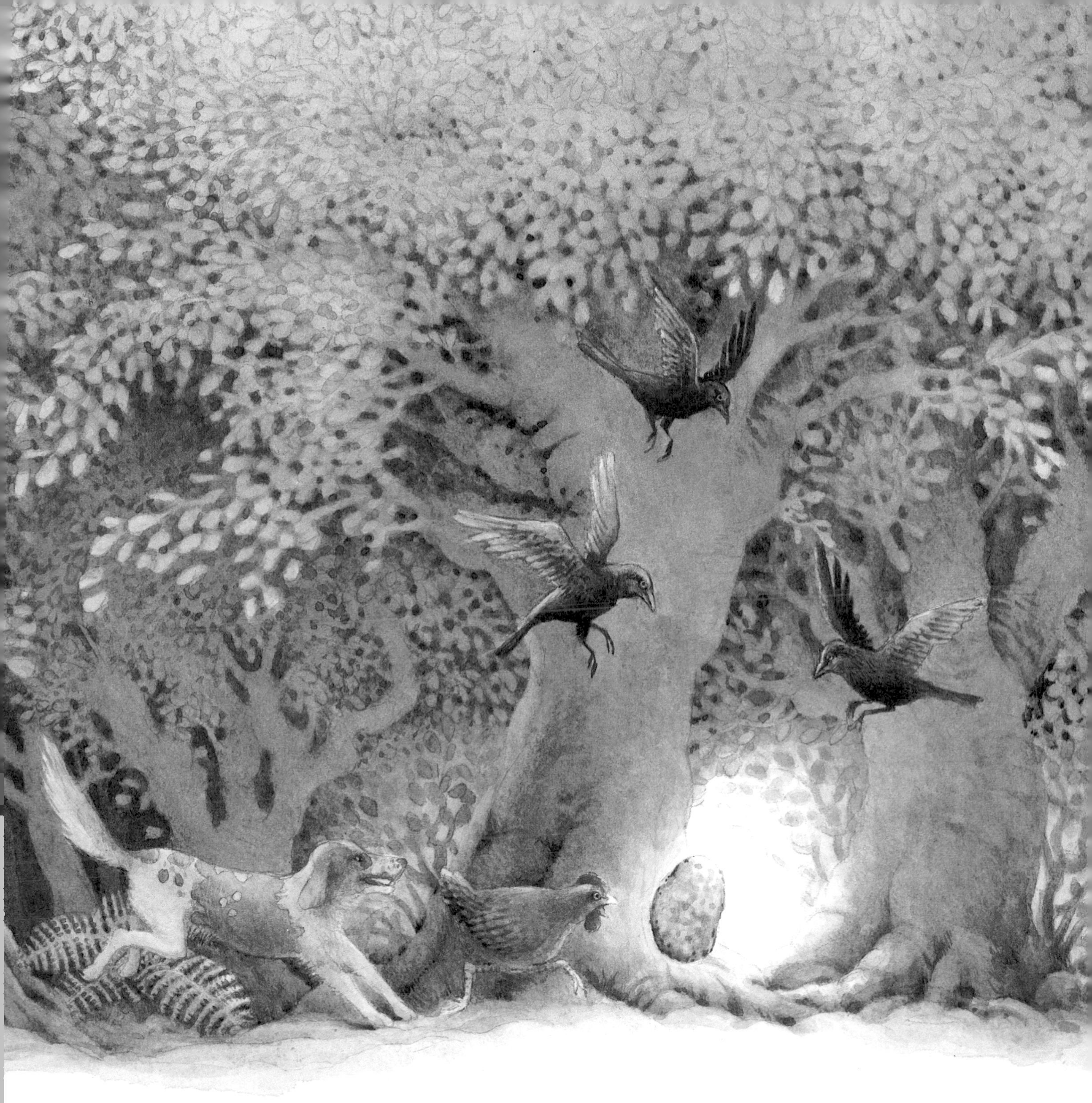

old ladies can't catch me, a little hen can't catch me, a dog can't catch me, a pig can't catch me, a goat can't catch me, and neither will you!"

And the pancake went on rolling faster and faster into the woods ...

… until it arrived where three children were getting ready for a picnic.
“Stop, you lovely fat pancake,” they cried. “We haven’t eaten a bite since lunchtime and we’re starving!”
So the pancake jumped straight into their hands, and they ate it up in a trice. Yum, yum, yum!